The Adventures of The Swamp Kids

A Zoo Ta-do!

Written by
Leif Nedland Pedersen

Layout and Illustrations by
Tim Banfell

Photography by
John Snell

Ally-Gator BookBites Publishing House

Published by
Ally-Gator BookBites Publishing House
1428 Watkins Street
Lake Charles, LA 70601
www.ally-gatorbookbites.com

Printed in the U.S.A. through Bolton Associates, Inc.
San Rafael, CA 94901
www.boltonprinting.com

First Printing
ISBN# 978-0-9886332-7-8

Our books are yummy!

Look for other titles and merchandise at
www.theswampkids.com

This book is dedicated to all of the kids, young and old, who made the magical trip up Monkey Hill just to slide back down to the bottom on their bottoms...
Keep on sliding!

Picture courtesy of Audubon Institute; circa 1963

Pierre hurried back from the mailbox one day

and the package he carried looked new.

"Come see what we got in the mail everyone,

it's the pictures we took at the Zoo."

The friends came together and circled around,

there was Plauche', Mon Cher and LaFleur;

and TuTu appeared as if coming from nowhere,

he wouldn't have missed this for sure.

"Remember how everything started that morning?

Our trip had a real stroke of luck.

Who knew Mrs. Buck Buck had eggs to deliver

and she'd let us ride in her truck?"

"Here's the first picture we took," said Pierre,

"in our trip that was filled with surprise.

We came to the Zoo having no expectations;

what we saw opened everyone's eyes."

"The first thing we came to was really amazing;

flamingos wherever you looked.

And wasn't it strange how they balanced their bodies

and stood there on only one foot?"

Plauche' said his favorite was also the biggest,

"The elephants really were cool;

I couldn't have guessed they would have their own fountain,

where TuTu had fun in their pool."

"Well, look at this picture of all of us posing,"

Mon Cher said while giving a laugh.

"It took quite an effort and working together

for us to all feed that giraffe."

"We watched the orangutans almost an hour,

they're such a big hit at the Zoo.

But while we were watching I couldn't help wondering

who is the one watching who?"

"Remember what fun we all had when we tumbled,
and ran up and down Monkey Hill?

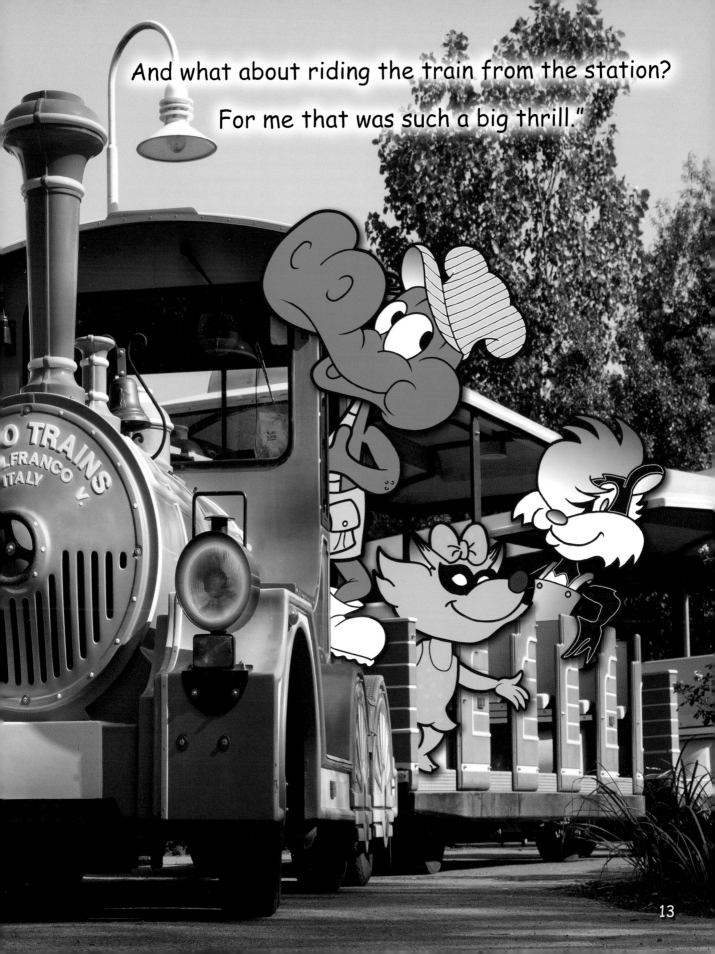

And what about riding the train from the station?
For me that was such a big thrill."

"I think that the cabin is what I liked best,

it reminds me of one that I knew."

He focused his glasses and suddenly said,

"It's my cabin that's on Bayou Bleu".

"You'll have to admit having lunch was a challenge,

the birdies and squirrels had a fling;

but soon they were calm and seemed to be listening,

when all of us started to sing."

A Diddle Ay Iddle Ayeeeeee,

A Diddle Ay Iddle Ayeeeeee;

We had a great day in a magical way;

A Diddle Ay Iddle Ayeeeeee!!!!!

"I wondered Pierre, when we went to the place

where the white alligators were seen,

if ever you thought you were seeing a cousin -

just none of his color was green?"

"I don't think he came from our Bayou, Lafleur;

I would guess he was brought here real young.

And what did you think when you saw the white tiger?

He saw us then stuck out his tongue!"

Then TuTu chimed in, "That was such an adventure;

it really was quite a big deal!

My only regret was I wasn't allowed

even once to go swim with the seals."

"I hope the next time we'll go see the Aquarium,

where all the fish are the show.

And maybe we'll stop by the new Insectarium,"

Mon Cher said, "I can't wait to go!"

Pierre said to all of them, "It was a pleasure,

to share this with you, my good friends.

To visit the Zoo and to see all their wonders -

a memory that never will end."

Lagniappe Lesson

By **Ron Forman**
President & CEO, The Audubon Institute

Hi kids and welcome to the wonders of Audubon Nature Institute...

This Swamp Kids adventure has taken you on a tour of many of the delightful exhibits located within Audubon Zoo, but did you know that we are much more than just a Zoo? Here's a look at some of the many things that make up Audubon Nature Institute:

Audubon Aquarium of the Americas and its adjacent Entergy IMAX® Theatre

The Aquarium is located at the foot of Canal Street at the Mississippi River and hosts more than 400 species, all housed in a realistic setting depicting the Great Maya Reef, the Amazon Rainforest, the Mississippi River expanse and the Gulf of Mexico. Entergy IMAX® Theatre is home to the largest IMAX® screen in the Gulf South. Located next door to the Aquarium, Entergy IMAX® Theatre combines the visual power of a five-and-a-half story screen with dynamic sound to put you in the middle of the action.

Audubon Butterfly Garden and Insectarium

Audubon Butterfly Garden and Insectarium, located in the U.S. Custom House on Canal Street, encourages you to use all five senses as you explore North America's largest museum devoted to insects and their relatives. You can even stand among hundreds of butterflies as they fly around you.

Audubon Louisiana Nature Center

Located in Eastern New Orleans, you become part of the wonders of nature in a natural setting. There is a network of nature trails and above-ground boardwalks that allow you to interact with the natural environment. Anticipated re-opening Winter 2015.

Freeport-McMoRan Audubon Species Survival Center

Behind the scenes, Audubon works to boost dwindling populations of disappearing animal species through expert animal care and innovative reproductive technology, with a critical mission to safeguard wildlife for future generations.

Become an explorer and find a zoo, aquarium, planetarium or some other facility where you live that brings you close to nature. You'll find there are wonders to behold...

Ron Forman

Audubon Nature Institute has its roots in historic Audubon Park, a natural setting for family recreation since the 1800s, and Audubon Zoological Gardens, which evolved from a single flight cage built in 1916 to a 58-acre jewel ranking among the nation's best zoos.

Ron Forman has helped guide the transformation of Audubon Zoo and the development of many new venues including Audubon Aquarium of the Americas and Audubon Butterfly Garden and Insectarium. As president and CEO of Audubon Nature Institute, Mr. Forman is a driving force behind the growth of this organization and stands as a community leader.

Our MANE Attraction

A statue you'll find of the king of the jungle, it's on Monkey Hill at the top.
Connect all the numbers and also the letters by drawing your lines to the dots.